STAR SEEKER

A Journey to Outer Space

Theresa Heine

Victor Tavares

Barefoot Books
Celebrating Art and Story

I'll hunt with Orion,
We'll stalk the dark night;
On the bridle of Pegasus
We'll trap a gold light.

With my lunar lasso
I'll loop Saturn's bright rings,
And brand all his moons
With the mark of the wind.

I'll bake ginger cookies
On Venus's soil,
Stir up her volcanoes
And watch them all boil.

I'll seize blue Uranus,
Then teach him to fly;
Like a Frisbee I'll fling him
Across the night sky.

I'll spin like a pinwheel
Through the Milky Way's froth,
Take a ride on the Great Bear
And never fall off.

With a zigzag of lightning
I'll spark Pluto's light,
And fireworks will blaze
On the planet of night.

I'll dive like an arrow

Past swift Mercury;

He's faster than thought

But he'll never catch me.

I'll steal Neptune's winds,
'Round his rings I will whirl;
Across his Dark Spot
Like a cyclone I'll swirl.

I'll swim across Jupiter's
Gigantic gas sea,
Then thread up his moons
On a necklace for me.

Like a comet I'll zoom
Over Mars's red crust,
And spy on his mountains
And valleys of dust.

From the bright Star of Evening
To Earth I will glide,
And drift through her gravity
Just for the ride.

I'll snooze on Earth's Moon
And when night is done,
I'll hitch up the North Star
And follow the Sun.

Explore Space!

Have you ever wanted to travel to outer space? If so, you're not alone. The sky has fascinated people for thousands of years. We've looked at the sky in wonder, hoping to understand what lies beyond the Earth, but the study of space is an ever-evolving science. Astronomers and scientists learn more and more about the planets and stars above us every day.

Ancient Mesopotamians, Egyptians and Greeks carefully studied the movements they observed in the sky. From these studies, the science of astronomy — the study of objects outside the Earth's atmosphere — was born.

The stars have been very important since ancient times for both navigation and for measuring time. For centuries, nomadic tribes, sailors and travelers have all used the stars to find their way at night. Farmers have depended on the movement of the Sun and stars and the changes of the Moon to know when to plant their fields.

In ancient Egypt, priests who studied the sky used their findings to predict the annual flooding of the River Nile. Central America created a calendar for keeping track of days both past and future. Even today, modern calendars include the phases of the Moon.

The Solar System

The solar system is thought to have formed from a cloud of gas and dust about 4,600 million years ago. It is made up of the Sun and all the planets, moons, comets and asteroids that move around the Sun.

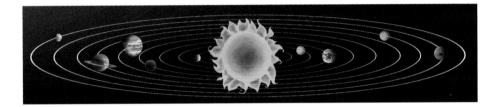

The **Sun** is the star that all of the planets revolve around.

A **constellation** is a group of bright stars forming a pattern.

A **planet** is a large body that revolves around the Sun.

An **asteroid** is a small rocky body that orbits the Sun.

A **moon** is a natural satellite that revolves around a planet.

A **comet** is a body of dust and gas that develops a long tail when nearing the Sun.

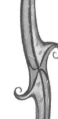

The Planets

There are nine planets in our solar system. Each planet orbits, or travels around, the Sun. It takes the Earth one day to rotate completely and one year to travel all the way around the Sun. The planets that are further away take much longer. Each planet also spins while it orbits.

I

Mercury is the planet closest to the Sun. It is the second smallest planet in the solar system. This planet is dense and rocky, and is covered with craters, mountains and valleys. In Roman mythology, Mercury was the messenger of the gods and wore a winged hat and sandals.

III

Earth is the planet we call home. It is the third planet from the Sun, and two-thirds of the Earth's surface is covered with water. Unlike the other planets, its name does not come from Greek or Roman mythology, but from the Hebrew word for "ground."

II

Venus is the planet closest in size to Earth. The surface of Venus is quite different, however. The temperature is very hot — it averages 427°C or 800°F! The entire surface is covered with huge volcanic craters. Venus is named after the Roman goddess of love, and is also known as the Evening Star.

IV

Mars is known as the "red planet" because of its blood-red surface, which is like a desert. Mars is a cold, dry planet, and can be seen from Earth without a telescope. It is named after the Roman god of war.

V

Jupiter is the largest and heaviest planet in our solar system. Earth would fit inside it 1,300 times! Jupiter is made up of gases and has no solid surface. Below its clouds the gas becomes a sea of liquid hydrogen thousands of miles deep. The Great Red Spot is Jupiter's most famous feature — it is a huge swirling storm like a hurricane and has existed for at least four hundred years. The planet has sixty known moons and is named after the ruler of the gods in Roman mythology.

VI

Saturn is known for its extraordinary rings, which are made of ice and ice-covered particles. It is the second largest planet in the solar system. Like Jupiter, it is a gas planet — it is so light that it could float on water, and you certainly couldn't land on its surface! In Roman mythology, Saturn was the god of agriculture.

VII

Uranus was the first planet to be discovered using a telescope. It is the seventh planet from the Sun, taking nearly eighty-four years to orbit the Sun once! Like the other gas planets, it is encircled by rings. The methane in its atmosphere absorbs red light, giving it its green-blue color. Uranus is named after the Greek god of the sky.

VIII

Neptune takes its name from the Roman god of the sea. It is very cold and dark, far out in the solar system — even in the fastest jet it would take two hundred years to reach it! It is another gas planet and has an enormous storm — the size of Earth — known as the Great Dark Spot. Its winds are stronger than those on any other planet. Neptune has four narrow rings made up of particles of dust.

IX

Pluto is the smallest planet in our solar system. It is normally the planet furthest from the Sun. The planet is a solid ball of rock and ice, and is always in the dark. In Roman mythology, Pluto was the god of the underworld.

The Sun, Moon and Stars

As well as the planets, the Sun, the Moon and the stars also fill our skies. A few of the constellations — recognizable collections of stars — are mentioned in this book, but there are many, many more to learn about too.

The Sun is the star at the center of our solar system. It is 4.5 billion years old! The Sun is the source of almost all of the Earth's energy. The temperature of the Sun's surface is so high that no solid or liquid can exist there. In ancient times, the Sun was used for telling time and differentiating the seasons. The Egyptians believed the Sun was a ball of dung pushed into the sky at dawn by a sacred dung beetle known as a scarab. The Romans called the Sun "Sol" and it was known in Greece as "Helios."

The Moon orbits the Earth every 27.32 days, and has a great influence on our planet. This is most obvious in the ocean tides, which are caused by the pull of the Moon. The Moon was called "Luna" by the Romans. The word "month" comes from "monath," the Old English word for "moon."

Orion is the brightest of the constellations, and is in the shape of a huntsman with a belt and sword. In Greek mythology, Orion was a great hunter. Artemis, the Greek goddess of the Moon, fell in love with him. Her brother Apollo (god of the Sun) did not approve and tricked Artemis into shooting Orion with one of her arrows. Saddened by his death, Artemis placed Orion's body in her Moon chariot and set him high up in the sky.

Pegasus was a winged horse in Greek mythology who became a constellation in the northern sky. Bellerophon, a Greek hero, attempted to fly with Pegasus to heaven, but was thrown from his mount when he angered the gods, falling back to Earth.

The North Star or Pole Star is at the very end of the long tail of the Little Bear (or "Ursa Minor"). Since ancient times, it has been important to sailors, caravans crossing the desert and other travelers who navigate by the stars at night. However, the North Star can only be seen from the northern hemisphere. In the southern hemisphere, the Southern Cross is used for navigation in a similar way.

The Great Bear or "Ursa Major," to use its Latin name, is a constellation that is most famous for containing the Plough, a constellation formed from its seven main stars. In Native American tradition, this constellation represented a hunter and his dogs chasing a bear. The ancient Egyptians considered the stars of the Plough to be part of the leg of a bull. In Arthurian legends, it was seen as King Arthur's chariot, and it has been described as a butcher's axe, a wagon and a saucepan.

The Milky Way is a galaxy, or very large group of stars. It is made up of more than a hundred billion stars! Our solar system is located within the Milky Way. The part of the Milky Way that is visible from Earth seems to form a great circle in the sky. The word "galaxy" comes from the Greek word for "milk," which is why our galaxy is known as the Milky Way.

For Till — T. H.

Jove is another name for Jupiter, the largest planet.
My 3-year-old son's nickname is Jove.
I dedicate this book to you, Jove — V. T.

Barefoot Books
2067 Massachusetts Ave
Cambridge, MA 02140

Text copyright © 2006 by Theresa Heine
Illustrations copyright © 2006 by Victor Tavares
The moral right of Theresa Heine to be identified as the author and Victor Tavares
to be identified as the illustrator of this work has been asserted

This book has been printed on 100% acid-free paper

Graphic design by Katie Stephens, Bristol
Color separation by Bright Arts, Singapore
Printed and bound in Singapore by Tien Wah Press Pte Ltd

This book was typeset in Koch-Antiqua, Rotis SemiSerif and Charlemagne
The illustrations were prepared in watercolors, gouache and airbrush

1 3 5 7 9 8 6 4 2

Library of Congress Cataloging-in-Publication Data
Heine, Theresa.
    Star seeker / Theresa Heine ; [illustrations by] Victor Tavares.
        p. cm.
    Summary: Describes an imaginary journey through the night sky, from joining Orion on a hunt to hitching
up the North Star for a ride. Includes facts about astronomy, the solar system, and constellations.
    ISBN 1-905236-36-0 (hardcover : alk. paper) [1.
Constellations—Fiction. 2. Planets—Fiction. 3. Stars—Fiction. 4.
Astronomy—Fiction. 5. Stories in rhyme.] 1. Tavares, Victor, 1971-
ill. 11. Title.
    PZ8.3.H4134325Sta 2005
    [E]—dc22
    2005019933

Barefoot Books
Celebrating Art and Story

At Barefoot Books, we celebrate art and story that opens
the hearts and minds of children from all walks of life, inspiring
them to read deeper, search further, and explore their own creative gifts.
Taking our inspiration from many different cultures, we focus on themes that
encourage independence of spirit, enthusiasm for learning, and sharing of
the world's diversity. Interactive, playful and beautiful, our products
combine the best of the present with the best of the past to
educate our children as the caretakers of tomorrow.

www.barefootbooks.com